Waiting for Adeline

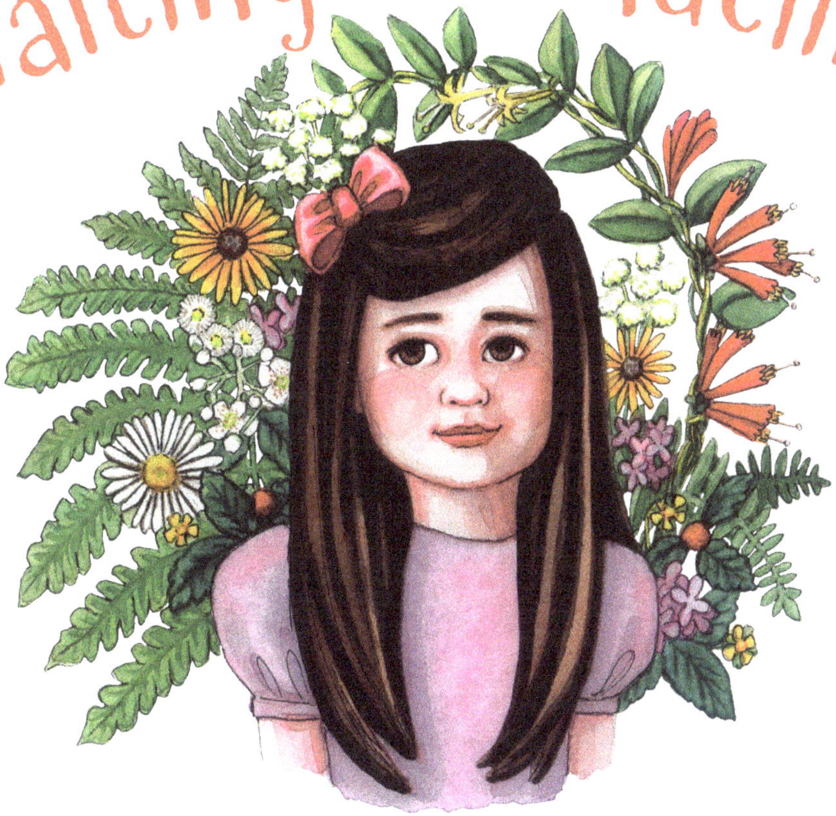

Story by
Lauren Oakey

Illustrations by
Britt Van Deusen

"This book makes me cry every time I read it. *Waiting for Adeline* is an honest, lovely portrayal of a child with developmental differences and the people who love her. An emotionally intelligent children's book, it creates room for the frustration and heartbreak that can go hand in hand with loving someone. Ultimately, it's a triumphant story about the bonds within a family and how there are ways beyond speech to communicate with the people you love."

—Robia Rashid, creator and executive producer of *Atypical*

Copyright © 2021 by Lauren Oakey

No part of this book may be reproduced in any form or by any electronic or mechanical means, or the facilitation thereof, including information storage and retrieval systems, without permission in writing from the publisher, except in the case of brief quotations published in articles and reviews. Any educational institution wishing to photocopy part or all of the work for classroom use, or individual researchers who would like to obtain permission to reprint the work for educational purposes, should contact the publisher.

ISBN: 978-1-953021-04-5
LCCN: 2021903913

Designed by Michael Hardison
Production managed by Haley Simpkiss

Printed in the United States of America

Published by
Belle Isle Books (an imprint of Brandylane Publishers, Inc.)
5 S. 1st Street
Richmond, Virginia 23219

BELLE ISLE BOOKS
www.belleislebooks.com

belleislebooks.com | brandylanepublishers.com

For Alice, Henry, Lynda, and Lucy

Some days . . .

Late on a summer afternoon . . .

A storm will blow in.

Not just a regular storm ... a derecho! It's a whirlwind of a storm! It comes quickly, out of nowhere, and pulls trees right up out of the ground.

The day that Mama and Daddy brought Adeline home from the hospital was one of those days.

Adeline was just like that tree-ripping storm—suddenly upon us, shaking our family by the roots and testing our strength to keep standing. All she ever did was cry! She cried and cried and cried all day long, and she cried all night too, so hard she couldn't sleep. Mama would sit next to her crib and sing to her, or rub her head, but nothing worked. That's when Daddy would hop on his horse to rescue her, like a true prince! He'd say, "Gimme that girl!" and plop down in his favorite chair in the den and hold her all night long.

I'm Alice, Adeline's big sister, but Mama and Daddy call me Bear. Mama says it's 'cause I was the easiest and sweetest baby she could have hoped for, cuddly like a teddy bear, and always happy to have a good nap. And just like a black bear, I also love to eat. Berries are my favorite!

Two years after me, my brother, Henry, arrived. He was always on Mama's hip, wrapping her long, drapey sweaters around his shoulders and smiling. Daddy said he was just like Mama on his insides too, so we called him Bones.

In our family, everybody gets a nickname. But with Adeline . . . we just weren't sure what to call her. I guess we hadn't quite figured her out yet.

In her quieter moments, Adeline would sit with her back against Mama's chest, facing out to see the world. She liked to track us, as Mama would say, watching us from one end of the room to the other and then back again. Bones could feel those big eyes on him between tears, so he'd dance around and sing to try and make her laugh.

(Some people, like Bones, offered to help with Adeline, but some of us had just had enough. I needed that girl to quit crying.)

After a while—a long while—Adeline did stop crying quite so much. Instead, she started babbling and fussing, pointing and making noise. But no matter what anyone tried, she could not get her words out. No words at all!

This didn't stop Daddy. He was determined that her first word would be "Dada." He would do things like jump on one leg and then the other, and chant "Da-da! Da-da!" to get her to say it. Of course, Bones joined right in. They were really quite the pair! But after all that jumping around, when Daddy said, "Adeline, where's Dada?" she would turn her head to look at him, but say nothing. Finally, he decided he was satisfied with that.

But not me. I wasn't satisfied at all. Why didn't she have anything to say? What was she waiting for?

The only person who had any real patience for all of this was Mama. When Adeline was hungry, she'd sit by the refrigerator, pointing and babbling so Mama could find what she wanted, and Mama would kneel down and watch her, like she was studying a book. Sometimes Mama couldn't guess right away, and Adeline would point and babble until she found it.

I liked to go up to my room at these times because the noise got to me, but Mama persisted. She'd say, "Bear, just because someone doesn't talk, doesn't mean they aren't thinking and feeling things. Sometimes, people who talk the least are the ones who say the most."

So, she'd wait for Adeline, in only the way Mama could.

But one day, Adeline was in the kitchen fussing at Mama, and you know what happened? I think Mama gave up. I truly do.

I'd barely made it to my room before the noise stopped. I tip-toed outta my room and went to the bottom of the steps, where I saw Mama on the front porch, sitting in the rocking chairs with Daddy. She had her eyes closed, and she was rocking slowly, back and forth, back and forth, and Daddy was holding her hand. I do believe Mama had put herself in Time Out.

I made my way past the porch toward the kitchen, and when I peeked in, I found Adeline at the counter, sitting in her chair with her head down, all alone and quiet.

I went to the refrigerator, pulled out the carton of raspberries I'd hidden way in the back, and went to the sink to wash them. When I turned around, Adeline's eyes had gotten real big, and she tracked me all the way from the sink back to the counter.

So, I sat down next to her and pushed the carton in front of her, and to my surprise, she gently laid her head on my shoulder and smiled. Adeline had wanted those raspberries all along. She just couldn't say it. And now, with her head on my shoulder, she was thanking me. (I guess Mama was right.)

So I said, "You're welcome, Baby Love."

And then I showed her my absolute favorite thing to do with raspberries. I put one on the end of each finger and pulled them off with my teeth. Boy, did she laugh!

After that, Mama and Daddy and Bones and me, we all started calling her Baby Love. And I started watching her, doing some tracking of my own. Here's what I learned:

When Baby Love leaned into Mama's leg, it meant she wasn't sure about something,

and when she reached up to Daddy, it meant she was scared.

When she crawled up into Bones' lap, she needed a place to rest, and when she grabbed her favorite blanket and hugged it, she was happy.

A step STEP, step STEP, step STEP in the morning meant she was coming downstairs for breakfast, and she was hungry (and there had better be blueberry muffins).

Her exclamation point was a giant JUMP into the pool, and a question mark was her head tilted just a little, watching a jar of lightning bugs light up in summer.

And when she touched her forehead to mine, or wrapped me in a giant hug and wouldn't let go, that was how she said, "I love you!"

And you know what? That's the best kind of love—the kind you don't talk about or give a name to.

You just know it's there.

About the Author

Lauren Tweel Oakey lives in Richmond, Virginia, and is a graduate of the University of Virginia, where she studied world religions and Italian language. She has lived in Italy and Switzerland, worked mostly in non-profits, and is a lover of language and the rhythm of words. She also enjoys playing piano, practicing yoga, and spending time with her husband, three children, and very beautiful but high-maintenance black lab. This is her first book.

About the Illustrator

Britt Van Deusen is an artist who lives in Richmond, Virginia, with her husband and three girls (two human and one canine). Britt studied painting at the College of William and Mary and the Marchutz School in France, and she has been a portrait artist for many years. When she is not making art, Britt often reads books that feature both people and animals in starring roles, regularly cooks somewhat fancy meals, occasionally plays silly songs on her guitar, and with stunning frequency, discovers birds' nests left abandoned in nature.

CPSIA information can be obtained
at www.ICGtesting.com
Printed in the USA
BVHW021958030921
615981BV00006B/529